Winston the Book Wolf

First published in Great Britain in 2006 by Bloomsbury Publishing Plc,
36 Soho Square, London, W1D 3QY

This paperback edition first published in 2007

Text copyright © Marni McGee 2006
Illustrations copyright © Ian Beck 2006

A CIP catalogue record of this book is available from the British Library

ISBN 9780747580133

Printed and bound in China by South China Printing Co.

10 9 8 7 6 5 4 3 2

All papers used by Bloomsbury Publishing are natural, recyclable products
made from wood grown in well-managed forests. The manufacturing processes
conform to the environmental regulations of the country of origin.

Winston the Book Wolf

Marni McGee

Illustrated by

Ian Beck

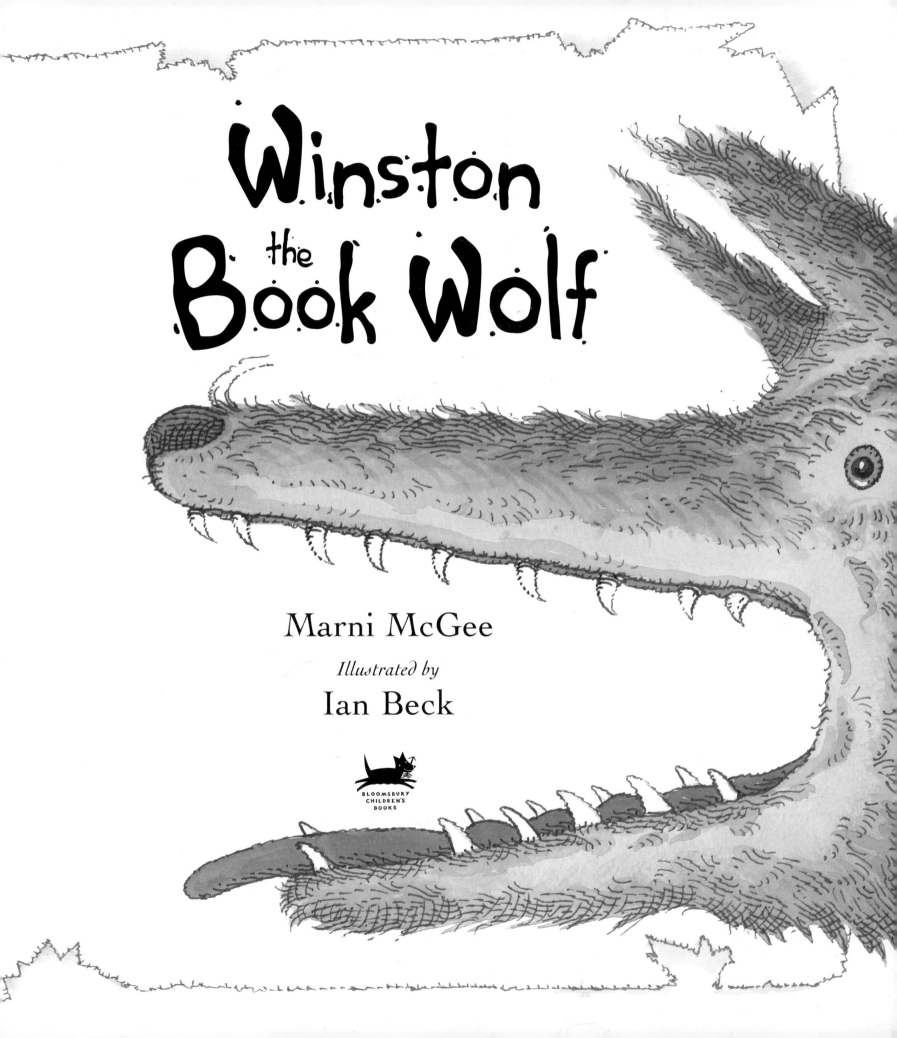

BLOOMSBURY
CHILDREN'S
BOOKS

Winston the Wolf swished his tail as he trotted past the burger stand. He *did* slow down to sniff, but he did not drool.

Meaty treats were not what
Winston had in mind.
Winston wanted **books** and
he knew where to find them.

He sauntered up the library steps and saw a handwritten sign.
"Words!" he exclaimed. "Yum!"

He snatched the sign and **ate it.**

The fierce librarian jingled her bell.
"He's back," she cried,
"that wicked wolf who chews on books!"

Library helpers came running. Winston tried to dodge them, but soon everyone was chasing poor Winston the Wolf.

Winston leaped over computers, hopped over tables and chairs.

Soon he'd be **trapped**.

But then a girl named Rosie appeared.
"Quick," she said. "Follow me."
Rosie showed Winston a secret door.

She led him through an alley, then under a bridge and over a hill.

When at last the two of them stopped, Rosie demanded the truth. "Why do you nibble on books? Why ask for trouble, Wolf?"

"Isn't it obvious? Can you not guess?" asked Winston. "Words are **so** delicious! Why, words taste better than roasted skunk, even better than gopher stew!"

"Wolf," said Rosie, "you must break this terrible habit. You must never nibble on books. Never again, do you hear?"

Winston began to howl. "I'll starve," he wailed. "I'll die without words!"

Rosie just laughed. "Oh, hush up, Wolf, and listen to me. You do *not* have to chew on a book to taste the lovely words inside. Words taste even better when you eat them with your eyes!"

Winston squinted at Rosie.

"Is this a trick? Can this be true?"

"Trust me," said Rosie. "Sit down. You and I are going to have lessons."

So each afternoon, Rosie read **stories** to Winston.
She taught him to sound out the words.
Winston caught on fast. He learned to eat words with
his eyes, which is to say: Winston learned to **read**!

The hungry wolf ate all sorts of words –
sweet and juicy words

like

sunset

and

swoosh

and rambunctious.

He wolfed down words like

trickle, icicle

and *twice*.

To him they tasted like clean, spring rain.

His favourite words rhymed with **crunch** —

punch and *munch* and *lunch*.

Winston read
Rosie's books until he
knew them all by
heart. Then
Winston said
to Rosie:

"I **must** have a
new stack of books."

Rosie sighed.
"Why try it again?
You know they
will bar the door.
The rule says:
NO WOLVES
ALLOWED!
You know
that means you."

"I'll never give up on books," he declared. **"Never!"** Then Winston smiled. "Do you suppose your grandmother's clothes might fit a wolf?"

Rosie scratched her head. "Grandma's clothes?"

"Trust me," said Winston. "I have a plan."

On Saturday morning at quarter to ten, Winston and Rosie walked to town. Winston wore a long, frilly, rose-print dress with ruffled lace at the neck. The skirt almost hid Winston's bushy tail and a floppy hat disguised his wolf-ly ears.

Perched on Winston's pointed snout were Grandma's specs in thin, wire frames.

When Winston and Rosie arrived, no one blocked the library door. Winston stuck his snout inside and breathed in the musty-dusty smell of books.

The librarian jumped to her feet and stared. That grandma looked familiar . . .

Rosie marched right up to her. "I'd like you to meet Granny Winston," she said. "She needs a library card so she can check out books. And she'll gladly read at Story Time – the children will love her tales."

Winston nodded.
"I'll read to the children all day long, if you like."

And so it was, week after week, "Granny Winston" read stories to children. If anyone noticed the sharp, white teeth, no one complained. And if at times the hem of Granny's skirt seemed to twitch and sway, no one revealed the secret.

Winston the Wolf – or Granny, so called – never lost his taste for words. Words were always and ever his favourite treat!

the
Story
Lady

A NOTE TO THE READER:
If your Story Lady wears long
skirts and floppy hats, she may
be a Wolf in Disguise – a lover
of words, a gobbler of books.
Please be very kind – for me!

Love,

Winston the Wolf x

Praise for *Winston the Book Wolf*...

'A wonderful twist on the *Red Riding Hood* tale.'
Junior

'A wonderfully original story with lots of classic characters.'
Angels & Urchins

'A boisterous book, with lots of mileage, it will inspire children to close their
eyes and imagine how their favourite words might taste.'
Daily Telegraph

'Ian Beck's illustrations . . . show Winston's world to be full of traditional
wonders, including the yellow brick road, a moon-jumping cow,
a cheeky blackbird, and three industrious little pigs.
This book should prove irresistible for Reception and Year 1 audiences.'
TES